Enid Blyton
Fun-time
Story Book

This edition first published in the United Kingdom in 1999 by
Brockhampton Press
20 Bloomsbury Street
London WC1B 3QA
a member of the Hodder Headline PLC Group

© Text copyright, Enid Blyton Limited
© Illustration copyright, Hodder and Stoughton Limited

Designed and produced for Brockhampton Press by
Open Door Limited
80 High Street, Colsterworth, Lincolnshire NG33 5JA

Colour separation: GA Graphics Stamford
Printed in Singapore

Title: Enid Blyton Funtime Story Book
ISBN: 1-84186-002-6

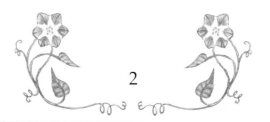

Enid Blyton

Fun-time Story Book

BROCKHAMPTON PRESS

Contents

 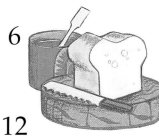

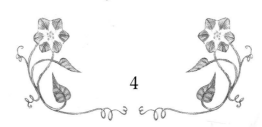

Contents

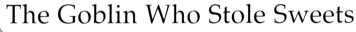

The Strange Doll

Doreen was very sad. She had a lovely baby doll that could shut its eyes and could say "Mama" quite plainly – and now the doll was broken!

It wasn't really Doreen's fault. She had put it on the table in the kitchen just for a moment whilst she went to get her doll's pram – and Mummy hadn't seen it there. She had put down a tray of dirty cups and saucers, and the doll had fallen off the table.

Crash! Her pretty face broke into pieces, and both her legs broke, too. Doreen was very much upset and cried bitterly.

"Oh, Mummy, can't she be mended?" she asked. But Mummy shook her head. "No, I don't think so," she said. "She is too much broken. I'm afraid I can't buy you another doll just yet, darling, because I really haven't the money. You must wait for your birthday."

"But that's ever such a long time away," said poor Doreen. "Oh Mummy, I shan't have a doll to take out in my pram now!"

Doreen put the broken doll in the pram cupboard. Then she put her pram away – but when she took hold of the handle, she thought she would go down the lane to the farm and back again, even though she had no doll in the pram to wheel along. She would just pretend!

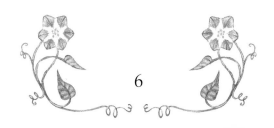

So off went the little girl, wheeling her empty pram. She went right down to the farm and then just turned to go back again.

Just as she turned, she heard a little whimpering noise. She looked round to see where it was. By the side of the lane, huddled under the hedge, was a puppy-dog. He was crying sadly all to himself.

Doreen went over to him. "What's the matter?" she asked. "Poor little puppy-dog, you are unhappy!"

The little dog whimpered again and did not move. "Come along!" said Doreen. "Come along! Don't sit under the damp hedge. Come out into the road and let me see you!"

But still the puppy did not move. So Doreen picked him up gently – and then she saw that he was hurt! One of his legs was bleeding, and he held it up as if it hurt him very much.

"Oh, dear!" said Doreen. "You're hurt! How did it happen? Did a farm-horse kick you – or a motor-car hurt you?"

The puppy whimpered again and licked Doreen on the face. He thought she was a dear, kind little girl. She put him down on the ground and tried to make him walk after her – but he was very much frightened, and would not move a step.

Doreen remembered that dogs have their names on their collars, so she took hold of his pretty red collar and looked at it. On it was printed: "White Cottage, Elmers End."

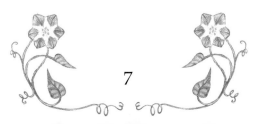

"Oh, you belong to Mrs. Harrison, who lives at Elmers End!" said Doreen. "Oh, dear – that's a long way away! I wonder if you can possibly get there."

The puppy yelped. He was trying to tell Doreen what had happened. His mistress had driven her car to the farm that morning and, just as she was leaving again, he had jumped out and hurt his leg. Now he was too frightened to do anything at all.

"However can I get you back?" said Doreen, patting the soft little head. "Oh! I've got such a good idea! I'll put you in my doll's pram, puppy! My doll broke this morning, poor thing, and the pram is empty. You'll fit in there nicely, because you are so small. I think I can manage to walk all the way to Mrs. Harrison's."

She picked up the puppy dog and put him gently into the doll's pram. He snuggled down on the pillow happily. It felt like his soft basket at home! Doreen pulled the covers over him and told him to go to sleep.

And so tired and frightened was the poor little puppy that he really did close his eyes and fall asleep in the pram! Doreen was so pleased.

"It's almost as good as having a doll!" she thought. Off she went, wheeling her pram carefully so as not to wake up the sleeping puppy-dog.

It was a long way to White Cottage where Mrs. Harrison lived. The little girl's legs were very tired long before she got there, but she didn't stop for a moment. She did so badly want to get the puppy back to his home and tell Mrs. Harrison to bathe his leg and wrap it up.

At last she came to White Cottage. Mrs. Harrison was in the garden, cutting roses. She looked up in surprise as she saw Doreen wheeling her pram up the path.

"Good morning, dear!" she called. "Have you come to show me your baby doll? What a long way you must have walked! You look quite tired!"

She went over to the pram and peeped inside – and how astonished she was to see a sleeping puppy there – her own puppy too! She stared and stared!

"Why, it's Sammy!" she said. "I thought I had left him behind at the farm and I was going to fetch him this afternoon!"

"I found him just near the farm, with a hurt leg," said Doreen. "I hadn't a doll in my pram to-day, because it got broken this morning. I was very sad about it because Mummy said it couldn't be mended, and she can't buy me another doll till my birthday. So I took my pram out empty – and it was a good thing I did, really, because, you see, when I found poor Sammy, I could put him into the empty pram and wheel him all the way home to you. I think his leg wants bathing and bandaging, Mrs. Harrison."

What a to-do there was then! The puppy woke up and tried to jump out of the pram when it saw its mistress. Its leg hurt and it yelped. Mrs. Harrison called for warm water and an old handkerchief – and soon the little dog's leg was well

bathed and had a nice clean bandage on. He really looked quite proud of it.

"Well, now, my dear, it really is time for your dinner," said Mrs. Harrison, looking at the clock. "Good gracious! It's past one o'clock! Your mother will be worrying about you. I'll run you and your pram home in the car."

She took out her little brown car and popped the pram into the back seat. Doreen sat in the front and in a very little while they were back at Doreen's home. Mrs. Harrison explained to Doreen's mother how kind the little girl had been.

"She tells me her baby doll was broken this morning and that was how it came about that her pram was empty and she could take Sammy back to me," said Mrs. Harrison. "I was sorry to hear about her doll. Do give it to me, Mrs. White, for I am sure I can get it mended for her. I know a doll's hospital in the next town. I can get a nice new head and two new legs put on, I'm sure."

She took the doll away with her and – will you believe it – in three days she brought it back again, quite better! It had on a lovely new head, just as nice as the first one, and two beautiful fat legs. The doll smiled at Doreen, who hugged it and kissed it in delight.

"Oh, thank you, Mrs. Harrison!" she said. "You are kind!"

"Well, you were kind first!" said Mrs. Harrison, with a smile. "It's funny how things happen, isn't it? Your doll got broken – so you took your pram out empty – and found Sammy and put him into it – and I was pleased, and heard about your broken doll and wanted to get it mended for you! So your bit of kindness has come back to you and made you happy! I'm glad!"

But the gladdest person of all was Doreen, as you can guess!

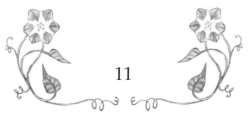

11

"Do Pass It On"

There was once a boy who liked doing kind things, and whenever people said to him – "It *is* kind of you to help me. Now what can I do for you in return?" – what do you think he said to them?

He said, "Oh, do pass it on! I don't want anything in return – just pass my bit of kindness on to somebody else. That's what my mother says we should do if people are good to us – pass it on!"

Well, that was a funny thing to say, but it was a very good idea. And now, just listen to what happened to a bit of kindness that was passed on!

Harry, the boy who began the bit of kindness, helped the old apple-woman to pick up the apples that fell out of her basket one morning. The old dame tripped over the kerb and down she went, with her apples all over the road! Dear, dear! She was so upset!

But along came Harry, helped her up, picked up all the apples, polished them with a clean handkerchief, and set them neatly back into the basket.

"You're a kind lad!" said the old apple-woman. "What can I do to repay you for your kindness? Will you have an apple?"

blew it over the hedge. It was almost in the mud. The apple-woman ran to it, and caught it before it got dirty. The washer-woman was so grateful. "That's kind of you," she said. "Very kind indeed."

"Do pass it on then!" said the apple-woman, pleased. "You pass on that bit of kindness, and don't forget!"

So the washer-woman thought about it and watched for a chance to pass it on. And very soon her chance came.

A little girl came down the road, crying. The washer-woman called out to her: "What's the matter, little girl?"

"No thank you," said Harry. "Just pass my bit of kindness on, will you?"

And off he went. "Very well!" thought the apple-woman. "I'll pass that bit of kindness on. I'll just wait and see how I can do it."

So down the road she went with her load, and very soon she came to where a woman was hanging out clothes on her line. Just as the apple-woman went by, the wind took hold of a pillow-case and

"Oh, I've been home, but my mother's out and I can't get any tea," wept the little girl. "And I'm so hungry!"

"Poor child!" said the washer-woman. "Come along in, and I'll give you some bread and treacle. I've got a bit of kindness to pass on to-day!"

So the child sat down and ate a great piece of bread and treacle. "You are very kind," she said shyly. "I wish I could give you back some bread and treacle."

"I don't want it, child," said the washer-woman. "Just pass the bit of kindness on – now don't forget. Do pass it on!"

The little girl ran off, pleased. She thought it was a funny idea to pass a bit of kindness on, but she made up her mind that she would. Her chance soon came. She passed a cottage where Mrs. Kelly lived with all her children, and saw poor Mrs. Kelly at the door, looking very worried. "What's the matter?" asked the little girl.

"Oh, I heard my Johnny's fallen down in the next street, and his leg's hurt so much he can't walk home," said Mrs. Kelly. "I want to go and fetch him, but I daren't leave the other children alone in the house – they're so little!"

"Well, I've got a bit of kindness to pass on," said the little girl. "I'll mind them for you, Mrs. Kelly!"

So Mrs. Kelly ran off to fetch Johnny, and the little girl minded the children and played with them. When Mrs. Kelly came back with Johnny, she was very grateful.

"I'd give you a penny for your kindness but I haven't one to spare," she said.

"Oh, I don't want any payment," said the little girl. "But, Mrs. Kelly, do pass it on!"

"Pass what on?" said Mrs. Kelly in great surprise.

"My bit of kindness!" said the little girl, laughing, and she ran home.

Well, Mrs. Kelly thought she certainly *would* pass it on, and she kept her eyes open to see how she could do it. She didn't have a wait very long.

When she passed the park gates with her children, she saw the park-keeper looking very miserable indeed.

"What's the matter, park-keeper?" she said. "Is your wife ill, or something?"

"Oh no," said the man. "But I forgot to bring my tea with me this afternoon, and I'm cold. I wish I had a drop of hot tea to warm me up!"

"Oh, I'll send my Bobby to fetch it for you," said Mrs Kelly at once. "He knows where your house is."

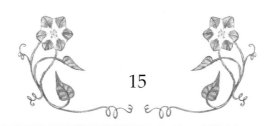

15

"What's up, Harry?" asked the keeper.

"My best ball's gone over the railings," said Harry. "I'm afraid someone else will find it in the morning. Then I shan't have it any more."

The keeper remembered the bit of kindness he had to pass on. "I'll go back to the park gates and unlock them for you," he said. "Then you can slip in and get your ball. What about that?"

"Thanks very much," said the park-keeper. "It's very, very kind of you. Anything I can do for you, by any chance?"

"No," said Mrs. Kelly. "Just pass it on, that's all!"

The park-keeper laughed. He promised he would, but he couldn't seem to think what to do. When six o'clock came, he rang the bell for everyone to go out of the park, and soon it was empty. He locked the gate behind him, and went on his way home, down by the park railings.

And just by the railings he saw a little boy looking upset. It was Harry, the one who began this story of passing on.

"Oh, I say, that is nice of you!" said Harry delighted. "But aren't you on your way home?"

"Oh, that doesn't matter," said the keeper. "I have got a bit of kindness to pass on, so perhaps this will do!" And back he went and unlocked the gates for Harry.

Harry got his ball and thanked the keeper. "Now just you pass that bit of kindness on!" said the keeper, smiling.

Well, wasn't it queer how Harry's own bit of kindness came back to him? He's busy passing it on again – and it may come to you this time. Do pass it on, won't you!

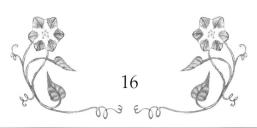

The Adventurous Ball

There was once a big round ball. It was all colours – red, yellow, blue, and green – and it looked very gay indeed when it bounced or rolled.

The other toys were rather impatient with the ball. They thought it a silly, dull creature. It could do nothing but bounce.

"What a life you lead!" said the sailing boat to the ball. "Nothing but bounce, bounce, bounce! Look at me! I go sailing on the river and on the pond. I even go on the sea at seaside time!"

"And what about *me*?" said the toy bus. "When I'm wound up I go round and round the nursery, and I carry dolls, bears, and rabbits for passengers! I have a fine life!"

"And I fly up in the air and see all kinds of things!" said the toy aeroplane.

"So do I!" said the kite. "I fly above the clouds and see the birds up there, and get as near to the sun as I can get!"

"And we dolls get about a lot too," said the curly-haired doll. "We go out in prams – we are taken out to tea – we do see the world! Poor, dull ball, you do nothing but bounce. We are sorry for you."

The ball felt sorry for himself, too. He had never felt dull before the toys had said all this to him, but now he really did feel as if he led a miserable sort of life.

However, the time came when all that was changed, as you will hear. It happened that the children in whose nursery the toys lived went off to the seaside for a holiday, and with them they took most of their toys. The bus went, the dolls went, the aeroplane, the kite – and the ball. What fun!

And then the ball's adventures began. It had longed and longed for adventures, and it was surprised when it had some. It had been taken down to the beach and left on the sand whilst the children dug castles. Nobody noticed that the tide had reached the ball. And no-one saw that it had taken away the ball when it began to go out again!

But it had! It bobbed the ball up and down on little waves, and took it right out to sea!

"Good gracious!" said the ball to itself. "I might be a little boat, the way I am floating along! Wherever am I going?"

A fish popped up its head and spoke to the ball. "Hello, big round fellow! What news of the land have you?"

The ball was proud to be able to tell news. It told the fish all about the other toys. Then the fish told the ball about the sea, and all the fishes and other sea creatures in it. "You are a bold, brave ball to go adventuring off by yourself like this," said the fish. "I do admire you!"

The ball bobbed on, prouder than ever. Soon a big white sea-gull swooped down and came to rest just by the ball. "Hello, big round fellow," he said in surprise. "I thought you might be food. How very bold of you to come adventuring on the sea like this!"

The ball felt proud – but it was a truthful ball. "Well, as a matter of fact, I can't very well help this adventure," he said. "The sea took me away."

"Tell me news of the land," said the gull. So the ball told all about the other toys, and the gull then told him of the gulls, and of their seaweed nests, and young brown gull-babies.

He told the ball of stormy days at sea. He showed him how he dived for fish. The ball was pleased and excited. How nice everyone was to him!

The ball bobbed in the pool and listened to the tales the crabs and shrimps told him He heard about the children who came shrimping with a big net. He saw how the little crabs could bury themselves in the sand in two twinks and not show even a leg. It was all very wonderful to the big ball.

When the tide went out again the ball went with it. It bobbed along merrily. Suddenly it saw a great big thing coming straight at it. Oh dear, oh dear – it was an enormous steamer! The ball felt sure it would be squashed to bits – but at the last moment it bobbed to one side and the big steamer sailed on. "Look! Look!" cried the people on the steamer, leaning over the side.

"There is a fine big ball, bobbing along all by itself!"

The ball was proud to be noticed by the people on the steamer. It bobbed after it for a long way but then got left behind. The tide took it once more and some great big waves curled over it and almost buried it. But it bobbed up gaily again; wondering what adventure it would have next.

As it floated along it saw a little boat with two children in. "Look! Look! There's a beautiful big ball!" cried the boy. "Let's get it!"

The ball floated on. The tide turned again and flowed into a big bay. The ball floated by a boat and stayed there for a while. The boat spoke to him and told him how he sometimes went out fishing and how little boys and girls went rowing in him and used him for bathing. The ball had never known such a lot of things in his life. He would have stayed by the boat for a longer time, but a little wave came and took him away. He floated into a rock pool, and there the crabs and shrimps swam up to him in admiration.

"What a fine big round fellow you are!" they said. "Where do you come from? How brave of you to adventure all alone on the big, big sea!"

The boat was rowed after the ball. The boy leaned out and took it. He shook the water from it and showed it to his sister.

"Do you know, Winnie, I believe it is our very own ball – the one we lost yesterday!" said the boy. "See the colours on it! I am quite sure it is our own ball!"

"So it is!" said the girl. "I wonder where it has been all this time! I wish it could tell us its adventures. I expect it has had such a lot, bobbing up and down on the sea."

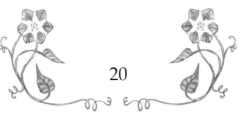

The children took
the ball back to shore. There
were all the other toys – the
aeroplane, the bus, the dolls, the kite,
and all the rest. How surprised they
were to see the ball again!

"We saw you floating away!" cried the
aeroplane. "Where did you go?"

"Ah," said the ball proudly. "I'm a big
round adventurous fellow, I am! I've
talked with birds and fishes, crabs and
shrimps – I've heard tales from boats
– I've nearly been run down by a great
steamer, and all the people on it saw me!
You may think I'm a dull fellow and can
do nothing but bounce – but you are
mistaken – I can float too – and I've had
more adventures than the whole lot of
you put together!"

And after that, as you can imagine,
none of the toys ever laughed at the ball
again for being a dull fellow who could
do nothing but bounce! He could tell
more stories than anyone else – and he
says he is going to float away again next
year and have some more adventures. I
wonder if he will!

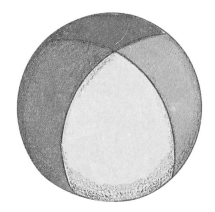

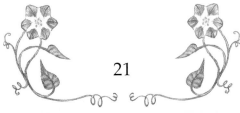

Enid Blyton

When Mrs. Tumpy Lost Her Head

Mrs. Tumpy lived in Peppermint Village in a little cottage called Toffee Roofs. She was a fat, round goblin woman, and all the elves, pixies and goblins in the village used to laugh at her because she fussed so much.

If one of her hens got loose she would run for miles asking anyone if they had seen it – and maybe it was under her henhouse all the while!

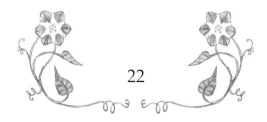

If she cut her little finger she would cry and scream, and somebody else would have to bind it up for her because she was so upset. And, dear me, one day when the wind caught her open umbrella and took her galloping down the village street, squealing for help, everyone thought she was being chased by robbers or something.

They came running out of their houses in fright. "Why, it's only that the wind has caught her open umbrella, like a ship's sail, and sent her scudding along," said Jinky, in disgust. "Hey, Mrs. Tumpy – leave go the handle and you'll be all right."

But Mrs. Tumpy was so scared that she quite lost her head. She wouldn't let go the umbrella handle, and the wind took her right to the duck-pond. She ran in at top speed and then sank. It took a long time to drag her out.

"Now, Mrs. Tumpy," said Jinky, when she was drying in front of his fire. "Listen to me. You fuss too much. You lose your head at the smallest upset. You are always making people think that something dreadful is happening to you, and all the time it's only a spider that has come out of a corner and made you jump – or something like that."

"Don't talk to me like that," said Mrs. Tumpy, crossly. "I won't have it."

"Well, you take my advice," said Jinky. "Don't lose your head too often – or one day it really will pop off and never come back!"

But Mrs. Tumpy took no notice of his words at all, and she still went on squealing at nothing, making terrible

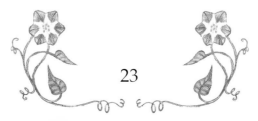

fusses, and calling for help if she saw even an earwig.

So Jinky grinned a little grin to himself, and made up his mind to give Mrs. Tumpy a shock. He went to his grandmother, Dame Know-a-Lot, and asked her for a disappearing spell. She gave him one in a box. It was blue powder.

"Whatever it's blown on will disappear," said Dame Know-a-Lot, It will still be there, of course, but no-one will see it. Take care how you use it, Jinky."

Now that afternoon Jinky walked quietly by Mrs. Tumpy's garden. He peeped over the wall and saw what he had expected to see – Mrs. Tumpy fast asleep in a deckchair.

Jinky smiled to himself. He jumped over the wall, and went on tiptoe to Mrs. Tumpy. He took out his box of blue powder and blew it gently over her head. Then he went back over the wall.

He stood and watched. Mrs. Tumpy's head gradually faded away and disap-peared. How peculiar she looked! Jinky could still hear her snoring. He tiptoed away, smiling.

Mrs. Tumpy soon woke up. She looked at her watch. Dear, dear, it was tea-time already. And Dame Quickly was coming to tea! Up she got and ran indoors. Soon she had the kettle on and went to the larder for the milk.

The cat had been there first. The jug was upset and the milk was on the floor. Mrs. Tumpy flew into a rage, and began to fuss around angrily.

"Oh dear, dear, dear! Now what shall I do? No milk, and there's Dame Quickly coming to tea. No time to get any more. Oh, where's that cat! Tabby, Tabby, Tabby!"

The cat came, but she didn't hear it. She turned to go to the stove and fell over it. Crash! She knocked her best teapot off the table.

"Oh, my, look at that! Nothing but bad luck today. Now what am I to do? Oh, goodness knows how I shall ever get the tea ready at this rate."

There was a voice outside the front door and Mrs. Tumpy heard the tap-tap-tap of Dame Quickly's stick as the old lady walked into the hall. "Now, now, Mrs. Tumpy, fussing again, and losing your head over something! Dear, dear."

Dame Quickly walked into the kitchen, and stopped in amazement, staring at Mrs. Tumpy.

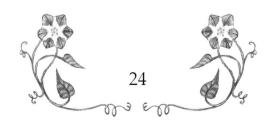

"What's the matter?" said Mrs. Tumpy, crossly. "Haven't I done my hair?" She turned to look at herself in the big glass – and then she gave a scream of dismay.

"Where's my head? I've lost it! Oh, mercy me, what's happened to my head?"

"Oh, Mrs. Tumpy, we always said you'd lose it if you went on like that," said Dame Quickly, "and now you have."

"Oh, oh – what shall I do? Where's my head gone?" wept Mrs. Tumpy, and tears from where her head ought to be fell down the front of her dress. She looked all round the kitchen, but her head wasn't there. She even went and looked into the larder, but of course it was nowhere to be seen.

She ran out into the garden. "Has anyone seen my head?" she called to the astonished passers-by. "I've lost my head! Has anyone seen it?"
Now most people guessed at once that someone had put a spell on Mrs. Tumpy to make her head invisible, and they laughed. But they weren't going to tell Mrs. Tumpy why. Oh, dear me, no! Perhaps if she thought she really

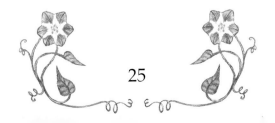

had lost her head, she wouldn't make such silly fusses as she did.

So everyone shook their heads, and said the same thing. "No, Mrs. Tumpy – so sorry, but we haven't seen your head anywhere. Dear, dear, we always said you'd lose it if you went on kicking up such a fuss about everything."

Poor Mrs. Tumpy couldn't eat any tea, or any supper either. She spent all the evening looking in the most unlikely places for her lost head. She even looked in the coal-scuttle and under the bed.

She went to bed very unhappy indeed. "I can't clean my teeth or brush my hair because my head has gone," she groaned. And then she was so tired out that she fell asleep.

In the night the spell wore off. When she awoke and looked fearfully at herself in the glass, how excited she was to find that her head had come back again. She smiled and nodded at it. "So you're back. Welcome home to me! I *am* glad to see you. And I do promise I'll never lose you again, dear head, never, never, never!"

And she was very careful after that not to lose her head or fuss when anything went wrong. So Jinky's mischievous little spell did some good after all.

26

Enid Blyton

The House in the Tree

Eileen and Marigold lived next door to one another, and they played together every day. But they were quite different!

Eileen was lazy and wouldn't bother about anything. Marigold liked to work hard, and would help anyone she could. Eileen was eight and Marigold was seven. Eileen couldn't read and Marigold could. Eileen didn't even know her twice times table, but Marigold had already got as far as four times.

Eileen laughed at Marigold because she liked doing things. "You are silly to learn to read," she said. "Your mother won't read to you any more now."

"Oh yes, she will," said Marigold, "and I'll be able to read to myself, too, so I'll get twice as many stories!"

"Well, I can always get my mother to read to me whenever I want a story," said Eileen. "So what's the use of bothering to learn?"

"You are lazy," said Marigold. "You can't even knit, as I can – you can't even tie a bow!"

"Well, you couldn't last week!" said Eileen.

"But I can now," said Marigold. "Look – I tied my own shoe-laces this morning – one on each foot. It took me a long time, but I did it. Now I can tie them every morning."

"Pooh!" said Eileen, scornfully. "I can get my mother to tie mine in half the time. What's the use of learning that if you've got someone to do it for you?"

Now one day, when Eileen and Marigold were playing in the wood, they heard the sound of someone squealing.

"Oooh! Oooh! Now look what I've done!"

Eileen and Marigold peeped round a tree to see who was squealing – and they saw a plump little woman sitting on a tree-trunk sucking her hand.

"What have you done?" asked Marigold.

"I was chopping wood for my fire when the chopper cut my thumb," said the little woman, her bright eyes twinkling at Marigold. "I shall have to bandage it."

"I'll do it for you," said Marigold. She took her clean hanky from her pocket and tore it into neat strips for a bandage. Then she quickly bound the little woman's thumb, and tied a neat little bow.

"What beautiful bows you tie," said the little woman, looking at her bandage. "Thank you very much. My goodness, my thumb does hurt. I don't believe I'll be able to dress my children for their party this afternoon!"

"Shall we help you?" asked Marigold.

"I don't want to," said Eileen, who was feeling lazy. "I want to play."

"Can you tie bows?" the little lady asked her, and Eileen shook her head. "Well, it's no use coming to help dress my children if you can't tie bows, because their party dresses have sashes – and they have to be tied in beautiful bows and each child has two plaits with bows at the end. So *you* wouldn't be any

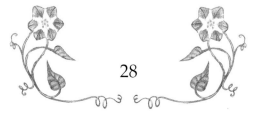

28

help. But this little girl would be a great help. Come along in, my dear!"

"Where's your house?" asked Marigold, looking round.

"In here!" said the little woman, and she pressed a bit of bark on a great oak-tree. A round door swung open! Marigold stared in surprise. So did Eileen. The little woman went in at the door and pulled Marigold in too. The door shut with a bang.

There was such a dear little room inside the tree. It was quite round. There was a

table in the middle and a wooden seat ran all round. Seven small pixie children were sitting on the seat, as quiet as mice.

"Oh!" said Marigold, "Your children are fairies!" "Yes," said the little woman, and she shook out a pair of wings from under her shawl. "I'm a pixie too, but I usually cover up my wings in the wood in case anyone sees me. Now, children – get your dresses!"

Each child opened a tiny cupboard beneath the seat where she sat and pulled out gossamer dresses. They were in two colours – blue and yellow. The blue dresses had yellow sashes and the yellow dresses had blue sashes. Each child had two pieces of hair ribbon to match her sash. They all wore plaits and looked perfectly sweet.

What a busy time Marigold had! She tied seven sashes into beautiful bows! She tied fourteen hair-ribbons into fourteen bows on the ends of fourteen little plaits! The children were as good as gold. Their mother was so grateful to Marigold.

"I suppose you wouldn't take the children to their party for me, would you?" she asked. "My hurt thumb really makes me feel rather ill."

"Oh, I'd *love* to!" said Marigold at once. "Where is the party?"

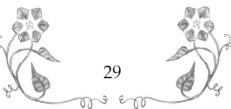

"It is at the Princess Silvertoes' palace in the heart of the wood," said the little woman. "The children know the way. Tell the Princess about my thumb, won't you, and say I'm sorry I cannot come. Good-bye, dears!" They all went out of the tree. Eileen was still outside, wondering what had happened to Marigold. When she saw her coming out with seven beautifully dressed pixies she was most surprised.

"I'm taking these pixies to a party at Princess Silvertoes', in the heart of the wood," said Marigold to Eileen. "Go home and tell Mother I will be a bit late."

"I want to come too," said Eileen in excitement. "Well, you can't" said the pixies' mother, standing in the doorway. "You didn't want to help me at all. You can't even tie a bow! You are a lazy, good-for-nothing little girl, and I don't want you to go with my children. Go home!"

So whilst Marigold went to the party and had a wonderful time, poor Eileen had to go home in tears. And I shouldn't be surprised if she learnt to tie a bow the very next day! I hope *you* can tie a bow – you never know when it will come in useful, do you?

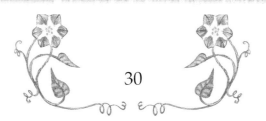

The Red-Spotted Handkerchief

Raggy the pixie had a red-spotted handkerchief that he was very proud of. It was a big one, with deep red spots all over it. Raggy always wore it in his front coat-pocket, where it stuck out a little so that everyone might see it.

Now one morning as Raggy was going along the road he wanted to sneeze. So he felt for his handkerchief to sneeze into – and it wasn't there!

Raggy was so surprised that he forgot to sneeze, which was a pity, for he really liked a good sneeze. He stood there feeling anxiously in all his pockets, but it wasn't in any of them.

"Somebody must have taken it!" said Raggy. "Yes – somebody at the meeting I've just been to! Oh how naughty of them! I'll go straight back and see who's got it! They will still be there talking."

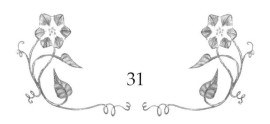

So back Raggy went and told everybody at the meeting that he had lost his red-spotted handkerchief.

"You lent it to Gobbo to wipe some spots off his coat," said Tag.

"But I gave it back!" said Gobbo at once.

"And you lent it to Hoppy to wave to his aunt when she passed by the window," said Tag.

"But I gave it back, I know I did!" said Hoppy. He turned out his pockets, and certainly there was no handkerchief there.

"And I lent it to *you*, Tag, to polish your silver watch-chain this morning!" said Raggy. "You must have kept it."

"Indeed I didn't!" said Tag. "I put it back into your pocket myself. Did you lend it to anybody else?"

"Yes, Raggy lent it to me to pop over my head when I went out in the sun to look for Jiggy," said Chuffle. "I tied a

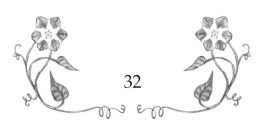

knot in each corner – but I untied them when I came back, and gave the hanky back to Raggy. I know I did. It's no use looking at me like that, Raggy. *I* haven't got your handkerchief!"

"Well, it's a very funny thing," said Raggy, feeling angry. "I seem to have lent it to all of you this morning, and I haven't got it myself – so *one* of you must have kept it! It's very mean of you!"

"Very well, Raggy, we'll all turn out our pockets and *show* you that we haven't got it!" said Hoppy. And everyone turned out his pockets for Raggy to see. There were sweets and tops and string and money – but no red-spotted handkerchief.

"Now you turn out *your* pockets, Raggy!" said Hoppy. "We'll make quite sure you're not making all this fuss for nothing!"

So Raggy turned out his pockets, but there was no handkerchief there either.

"It's not a bit of use," said Raggy! "*One* of you has my

beautiful handkerchief, and it's very wrong of you!"

"Now, Raggy, when you left the meeting, I *know* I saw your red handkerchief sticking out of your front coat-pocket," said Chuffle. "I just know I did. So if you took it away yourself, we couldn't have kept it! Did you meet anyone on your way home?"

"Well, go on," said Hoppy.

"And after a bit I saw a cow looking over a hedge," said Raggy.

"Did you lend *her* your handkerchief?" asked Chuffle.

"Really, Chuffle, do you suppose I go about lending cows my handkerchief?" said Raggy! "I suppose you think she wanted to polish her shoes with it? Well, she didn't!"

"Go on. What did you do next?" asked Hoppy.

"Well, let me see," said Raggy. "Oh, I know – a car came suddenly round the corner, and I had to jump quickly into the hedge – and I fell over and hurt my knee very badly."

"Did you really! Poor old Raggy," said Hoppy, for he knew how painful it was to fall down. "Did your knee bleed?"

"Oh, terribly!" said Raggy. "I had to bandage it…"

He suddenly stopped and went very red indeed. He didn't finish what he was going to say.

"Go on," said Tag.

"No, nobody!" said Raggy.

"Tell us exactly what you did," said Hoppy.

"Well," said Raggy, "I left the meeting, and walked up the road. I met a dog with a black head,"

"Did you lend *him* your handkerchief?" asked Tag.

"No, of course not," said Raggy. "What would a dog want a handkerchief for? To wave to the engine-driver of the train, or something? Don't be silly."

"Oh, that's all," said Raggy. "Well, I don't think I'll bother any more about my handkerchief. Good-bye, everyone."

"No, no, Raggy, don't go yet!" said Tag, and he held him by the arm. "Let's see your poor hurt knee!"

"Oh, it's quite all right now," said Raggy.

"It might not be," said Tag. "We'd better look and see if it wants bathing. Turn up your trouser leg, Raggy."

So Raggy had to, and his knee was neatly bound up with – what do you think? Yes – his red-spotted handkerchief!

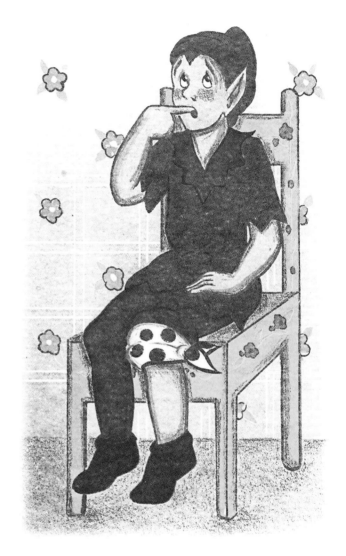

"I don't wonder you feel ashamed of yourself," said Tag sternly. "Coming back here and making all that fuss, when if only you'd thought for a moment you'd have known quite well where your silly old handkerchief was all the time!"

"I'm sorry," said Raggy, and he went home feeling very much ashamed. He didn't like to wear his handkerchief any more, so now it is neatly folded in his drawer. Silly old Raggy – he did make a mistake, didn't he?

The Little Toy Stove

Angela had a little toy stove. It was a dear little stove, with an oven that had two doors, and three rings at the top to put kettles or saucepans on. At the back was a shelf to warm plates or keep the dinner hot. Angela liked it very much.

But Mother wouldn't let her cook anything on her stove. "No, Angela," she said, "you are not big enough. I am afraid you would burn yourself if you lighted the stove and tried to cook something."

"Oh, but Mother, it isn't any fun unless I can cook myself something!" said Angela, nearly crying. But Mother wouldn't let her light the stove, so it was no use saying any more.

Now one day, as Angela was playing with her saucepans and kettles in the garden, filling them with bits of grass for vegetables, and little berries for potatoes and apples, pretending to cook them all for dinner, she heard a tiny voice calling to her.

"Angela! Angela! Do you think you would mind lending me your stove for this evening? My stove has gone wrong, and I have a party. I simply *must* cook for my guests, and so I wondered if you'd lend me *your* stove!"

Angela looked all round to see who was speaking. At last she saw a tiny elf, not more than six inches high, peeping at her from behind a flower.

"Oh!" said Angela in delight. "I've never seen a fairy before. Do come and let me look at you."

The elf ran out from behind the flower. She was dressed in blue and silver, and had long shining wings and a tiny pointed face. Angela thought she was lovely.

"Will you lend me your stove?" asked the elf. "Please say yes."

"Of course!" said Angela. "I'd love to. Will you really cook on it? My mother won't let me."

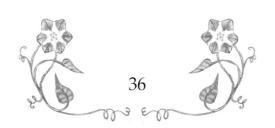

"Of course she won't let you," said the elf. "You aren't big enough yet. You might burn yourself."

"Shall I leave my stove here for you?" asked Angela.

"Yes, please," said the elf. "I can easily cook out here. It is to be an open-air party. I live behind those hollyhocks, so I shan't have far to bring my things."

"I suppose I couldn't come and watch you?" said Angela longingly. "I've never seen my toy stove really doing cooking, you know!"

"Well, you come and watch to-night," said the elf. "I shall begin my cooking at nine o'clock. The party begins at eleven."

Angela was so excited when she went in to bed. She meant to put on her dressing-gown and get up at nine o'clock, and creep down the garden.

So she lay awake until she heard the hall clock chime nine. Then up she got and slipped down the stairs and out of the garden door.

She could quite well see where her toy stove was, because smoke was rising from it. The elf had got it going well. A lovely smell of baking and roasting came on the air. Oooh!

You should have seen the elf cooking on that stove. The oven was full of things roasting away well. The plates were getting nice and hot in the plate-rack!

"Just listen to my pudding boiling away in that saucepan," said the elf, pleased. "This stove cooks very well indeed; it's a fine stove."

"What sort of pudding is it?" asked Angela.

"It's a tippy-top pudding," said the elf. "And I'm cooking a poppity cake too and some google buns."

"Oh my, they do sound delicious," said Angela, "and so exciting! I've never heard of them before. I suppose I couldn't come to the party?"

"No," said the elf. "It is too late a party for little girls like you. But, Angela, as I think it is really very kind of you to let

me use your lovely stove for my cooking, I'd like you to taste some of my dishes. Listen! There is sure to be some tippy-top pudding, some poppity cake, and a few google buns over after the party. If there are I will put them on a plate and leave them inside the oven. See? I will clean the stove nicely, too, and leave it all shiny and bright. Now, good night, dear. You must go to bed. You are yawning."

"Good night!" said Angela, and she ran off. In the morning she went to see if there *was* anything inside her oven. And what do you think? There was a neat little blue dish, and on one side of it was a slice of yellow tippy-top pudding, and on the other side were three google buns, red and blue, and a large slice of green poppity cake! Ooooh!

Angela ate them all – and they were simply delicious. She *does* so hope the elf will want to borrow her stove again. Wouldn't it be lovely if she did?

Enid Blyton

The Proud Little Pig

There was once a little pig who was very proud. He lived with his brothers and sisters in a sty in a farmyard, but he didn't like them at all.

"You are all so *stupid*," he said to his family. "Why, you can't even say 'Boo!' to the old goose who comes and looks at us through the gate."

"Why *should* we say 'Boo'? asked his mother, who was large and fat and round.

"Because that is what people always do say to a goose," said the little pig. "I'm surprised you don't know that."

"Don't be cheeky," said his mother, and she poked him with her big snout so that he rolled over in the mud. He was very angry.

"I don't like belonging to this family," he said in a grunty voice, turning up his nose at everyone. "What do you do all

40

day long? Eat and gobble, gobble and eat! Greedy fat creatures!"

"Well, really, Piglet, you shan't talk like that!" said his mother, and she caught hold of his very curly tail and bit it hard. How the piglet squealed! He tore round and round the sty, trying to lick his tail, but he was so round and fat that he couldn't bend far enough.

"I shall not live with you any more!" he said to his family, who stood grunting with laughter at him. "I shall pack my bag and go and live with someone who is far wiser and cleverer than any of you. I am wasted here! Good-bye!"

And off he went, taking his little bag with him, with his toothbrush, sponge, and winter scarf inside.

"Where are you going?" grunted his mother.

"I shan't tell you!" said the pig. And indeed, he *couldn't* tell her, because he didn't know himself.

As he trotted along, carrying his bag in his mouth, he thought hard. "I must think of a good clever name for myself," he said. "Piglet is a stupid name. I will call myself Mr Grunt. That sounds grand."

So Mister Grunt scampered on and on and at last he came to a wood. He crept under a bush to rest, and there he found a hole leading deep underground. He sniffed down the hole and knew that someone lived there. So he called down:

"Who lives here?"

"Mister Reynard the Fox," came the answer.

"Who's that at my front door?"

"Mister Grunt," said the piglet in a haughty sort of voice. "Are you a clever person, Mister Reynard? I have left my family and am looking for a really wise person to live with."

The fox grinned. He knew quite well that Mister Grunt was a pig, for he could smell him.

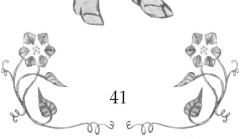

"You are nice and fat," said the fox.

"I am very wise," said the pig.

"You are the plumpest pig I have ever seen," said the fox.

"I have left my family because they were so stupid," said the pig.

"I am simply *longing* for my dinner," said the fox, and he looked at the pig in such a queer way that he was quite alarmed.

"Come along in, Mister Grunt," called the fox. "I'm sharp enough, as anyone will tell you – and I'd like someone smart to live with me and keep me company."

So down the hole trotted the pig, with his little bag. He didn't much like the smell, because it was even stronger than his own pigsty. He bowed to Mister Reynard, who licked his lips when he saw the fat little pig.

"How do you do?" asked the pig. "I am a clever pig."

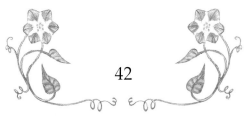

path went up it, so the pig went up it too. He was soon panting and puffing, and his bag seemed very heavy. He made the curl in his tail as stiff as he could, and hung the bag on that. It was so difficult to pant and puff with a bag in his mouth.

Now, at the top of the mountain, hidden away in the rocks, was the nest of two big eagles. They had young ones in the nest, and they fed them every day with rabbits, small birds, and other creatures.

The pig came to the nest, and stopped in surprise when he saw two big eagles sitting quietly there, their hooked beaks turned towards him, and their sharp eyes gleaming.

And then he heard a rabbit's voice calling down the hole warningly:

"People who go down this hole don't come back! Beware!"

Well, that was quite enough for the pig. Before the fox could grab him, he scuttled backwards up the hole and rolled over on the bracken outside. In a trice he was away, scampering through the wood. The fox didn't go after him, for he disliked hunting in the sunlight. It hurt his eyes.

The pig ran for a long way. At last he came to a very steep hill. It was a mountain, but he didn't know it. The

"Good morning," said the pig. "I am Mister Grunt, a very wise pig. Are you clever too?"

"Very," said one eagle "Of course," said the other.

"Well, perhaps you would like me to live with you then," said the piglet eagerly. "I have left my stupid family, and I am looking for a new home with wise folk."

"You are very fat, Piglet," said the first eagle. "As plump as can be, Piglet," said the other.

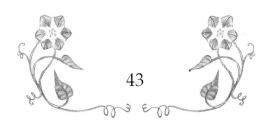

43

"My name is Mister Grunt," said the pig in rather a haughty way.

"You are deliciously round," said the first eagle, and his beak snapped open and shut.

"You would make the finest dinner in the world, Piglet," said the second eagle dreamily. "Come nearer."

The little pig was alarmed. Good gracious. Here was someone else wanting to eat him!

He galloped over the top of the mountain with his bag, caught his foot in a root, and rolled over and over and over and over till he came to the very bottom at the other side!

Goodness! He had no breath left, and he felt bruised all over. He lay where he was for a moment, and then, seeing two big specks flying in the sky, he got up quickly. He was sure the two specks were

44

the eagles looking for him! He hurried away as fast as he could.

"It's too bad," he thought. "Too bad! Why must all the clever people I meet want to eat me? They seem to think more of my body than of my brains. It's too bad!"

Now at last he came to a house, built by a running stream. It looked a nice cosy house, and smoke came from the chimney. There was a sound of talk and laughter inside, and the little pig felt that here, perhaps, he could make his home.

So he knocked timidly on the door.

"Come in!" cried half a dozen voices. He went in. He saw a family sitting round the table – a mother and father and four children, all merry and bright eyed.

"Good-day," said the pig. "I am Mister Grunt. I have left my stupid family and I would like to live with a clever one. You look very clever to me."

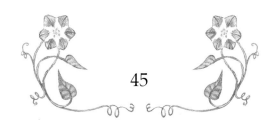

"Oh, we are, we are!" they all cried. "Shut the door Mister Grunt and come along in."

"I have a lot of brains," said the pig, pleased to be welcomed like this. "I would make good company for you."

"We are sure of it!" cried the family. "You look very wise and smart."

The pig was really delighted. His tail curled more tightly than ever, and his snout lifted high in the air.

"I will live with you," he said. "May I join your meal? I am very hungry, for it is a long time since I left my sty."

"Of course!" said the father, and he set a chair for the pig. We have a lovely dinner to-day. We are eating a dish of sausages."

SAUSAGES! SAUSAGES! The little pig looked at the family in horror! Hadn't he heard his mother say that naughty pigs were made into sausages?

Oh dear, oh dear, oh dear! This was worse than anything he had heard that morning!

Picking up his bag he fled out of the door, as fast as ever he could, not even stopping to shut it. Sobbing and crying

the proud little pig trotted along, trying to get as far from the house as he could. If only he had never left his nice, comfortable, safe pigsty!

He wandered on for miles, and suddenly he heard the sound he knew. It was Rover, the old farm-dog, barking!

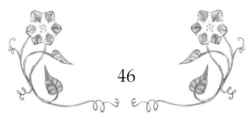

46

The little pig had found his way home again, and there he was, outside his farmyard! He trotted in and went to the sty.

"Mother!" he yelled. "I've come back again."

"Snouts and tails!" said his big mother in surprise. "I thought you were too clever to live with us!"

"Oh, Mother. I made a mistake," said the pig. "I was very stupid to go out into the big world, for there everyone wants to eat me. But here I am safe, and I think it is better for a pig to be stupid and safe than clever and eaten!"

"Come under the gate then," said his Mother. "And don't let us hear any more about being clever."

So under the gate he went, and never once did he grumble again at his family. But do you know, he had such a fright that all the curl come out of his tail. So if you go to a pigsty you'll know which is Mister Grunt, won't you? – the pig with the very straight tail!

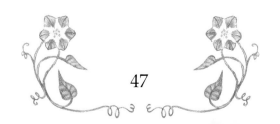

The Pantomime Cat

"Mollie! John!" called Mummy. "Where are you? I want you for a minute."

The two children were playing out in the garden. They ran in.

"I hear that old Mrs. Jones isn't well," said Mummy. "She can't go out and do her shopping. Now I think it would be very nice if you two children did her errands for her each day until she is better."

"Oh, Mummy, I don't like Mrs. Jones!" said Mollie. "She always looks so cross!"

"And she never gives anyone a penny, or a biscuit, or a sweet, or anything," said John.

"You don't do kind things for the sake of pennies or sweets," said Mummy. "You know that. You do it because it is good to be kind. You like me to be kind to you?"

"Yes," said Mollie. "We love you for it, Mummy! All right. We'll go – won't we, John!"

They were good- hearted children, so each day at ten o'clock in the morning they ran up the hill to Mrs. Jones's little cottage, knocked on the door and asked her what errands she wanted running.

Mrs. Jones never seemed very pleased to see them, and certainly she never gave them anything, not even a sweet out of her peppermint tin. She was not a very kind old lady and, although the children were polite to her, and always ran her errands cheerfully, they thought she was a cross old thing, and were glad when they had finished going to the grocer's, the baker's and the fishmonger's each day.

It was the Christmas holidays, and circuses and pantomimes were in every big town. There was a pantomime in the town where Mollie and John lived too, and children often stopped outside the big theatre and looked at the pictures.

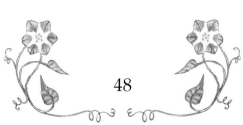

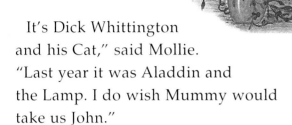

It's Dick Whittington and his Cat," said Mollie. "Last year it was Aladdin and the Lamp. I do wish Mummy would take us John."

But Mummy had said no, she hadn't enough money for all of them. Perhaps they would go next year.

"You said that last year Mummy," sighed Mollie. "I do wish we were rich! I'd love to go every night and see Dick Whittington and his clever cat. A girl I know has been, and she says the cat is ever so big and so funny that she laughed till she couldn't laugh any more!"

"Now it's ten o'clock," said Mummy. "Off you go to Mrs. Jones. You won't have to do her errands much longer because she can walk quite well now. You have been good children to run them so cheerfully."

Off went Mollie and John up the hill. They knocked at Mrs. Jones's door and went in. She was sitting at the table, sewing something with a big needle.

The children looked at it. It was a strange thing she was sewing – like a big, black fur rug – with a cat's head. "Whatever is that?" asked Mollie, in surprise.

"Always asking questions!" grumbled the disagreeable old woman. "It's the cat skin my son wears in the pantomime. Didn't you know he was the Cat in Dick Whittington this year?"

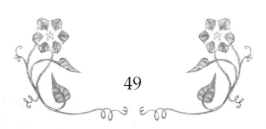

49

"Oh, no!" cried both children in delight. "How perfectly lovely!"

"Hmmm!" said Mrs. Jones, snapping off her thread. "Not so very lovely, I should think – nasty hot thing to wear every night for hours on end. Hmmm! Now listen – my son wants this cat costume this morning before eleven, so pop down now straightaway and say you've brought his costume. That's all I want you to do to-day. After this morning I can do my own shopping, so I won't be seeing you any more."

She wrapped up the parcel and the children sped off. "Mean old thing!" said Mollie. "Never even said thank you to us! I say! What fun to be going in at the stage door of the theatre! We might see some fairies – you know – the ones that sing and dance in the pantomime!"

They soon arrived at the stage door and asked the old man there for Mr. Jones.

"Go up the stairs and knock on the second door on the right," said the old

chap. Mollie and John ran up the stone steps and knocked on the second door.

"Come in!" shouted someone – and in they went.

A round, jolly-faced man was sitting in front of the mirror. He smiled when he saw them. "Hallo!" he said. "Have you brought my cat skin? Thanks awfully! I say are you the two children who have been running errands for my mother all this time?"

"No, we haven't," said John. "Mummy can't afford to take us this year – but, oh, you must look lovely! I wish we could see you!"

"Well, you shall!" said the jolly man, unwrapping the parcel. "You shall have free tickets every night of the week, bless your kind little hearts! That's your reward for being kind to someone who never said a word of thanks! I've some free tickets to give away – and my mother never wants to use them – so you shall have them! Would you like that?"

"Oh, yes!" shouted the children, their faces red with delight. "Yes, yes, yes! We shall see Dick Whittington – and the fairies – and you – and everything else! Oh, what luck!"

Well, it all came true – they did see the pantomime, every night of the week! The jolly man gave them their tickets and, oh, how they loved every minute of it!

"Yes," said Mollie shyly.

"And I guess she never said thank you did she? Or gave you a penny between you," laughed the man. "She's a funny old thing, but she means well. Have you seen me in the pantomime, dressed up in this cat skin?"

"The cat is the best and funniest of all!" said Mollie and John. "We do love him! And we are proud of knowing him, Mummy! Fancy knowing the pantomime cat! All the other boys and girls wish they were us!"

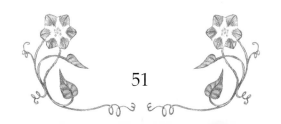

"Ah! You didn't know you were running errands for the pantomime cat's mother, did you?" said Mummy. "You never know what will happen when you do a kindness!"

The Goblin Who Stole Sweets

Somebody was stealing sweets out of the toy sweet-shop in the nursery! There were twelve bottles of sweets there – and every day some of them disappeared.

"*I'm* not stealing them!" said Teddy bear.

"And I wouldn't touch *one*," said the toy soldier, though he was very fond of sweets.

"Well, someone's stealing them," said the Dutch doll. "And what Janet and Ronnie will say when they find out that their toy-shop sweets are gone, I really can't think!"

"We must find out who is taking them," said the blue rabbit. "They disappear in the afternoons, when the children are out for their walk and we are shut up in the toy-cupboard."

"Well, this afternoon we will take the key of the cupboard away, so that Nanny can't lock the door!" said Teddy. "Then we'll creep out and see who is the thief."

So that afternoon, when Janet and Ronnie had gone out for a walk, and had left the toys in the cupboard, they all crept out and hid in different places in the nursery, so that they might watch for the robber.

The toy soldier sat up on the nursery window-sill behind the curtain. He looked out of the window.

"Ooooh!" he said. "It's snowing! There is a white carpet all over the ground. I can see all the way down the hill, and there's snow everywhere. I wish we could toboggan!"

"Sh!" said the blue rabbit. "Somebody is coming!"

And sure enough somebody was! It was a little green goblin, with a long nose and ears, and naughty eyes. He slipped in at the door, and ran to the toy sweet-shop. In a trice he picked up two of the bottles of sweets, and was just going to uncork them when the toy soldier shouted at him:

"Stop, thief! You naughty robber! Put down those bottles at once!"

The goblin jumped. He looked round – but when he only saw toys watching him, he grinned.

"Shan't!" he said.

"You jolly well will!" said the teddy, and he rushed at the goblin. But quick as lightning the little green fellow ran to the door and out. He slipped into the garden and ran to the gate. Then,

staggering about in the thick snow, he began to go down the white hillside with the two bottles of sweets.

"He's taken two whole bottles!" said Teddy.

"Stop him!" said the blue rabbit.

"How?" asked the Dutch doll, very worried.

Come on, I'll show you!" yelled the toy soldier suddenly, and with one leap he was down from the window-sill. He caught up the tin nursery tray and rushed outside, followed by all the rest of the toys. They ran to the gate quite easily, for the snow had been swept away from the path.

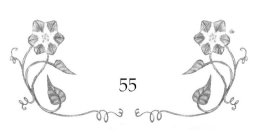

"But how can we get down this snowy hill?" asked the Dutch doll, in dismay.

"That's what I brought the tray for – to get down the hill before the goblin does!" cried the toy soldier, and he slammed the tray on the snow at the top of the hill. "Get on, everyone."

They all got on, though the blue rabbit was very much afraid. The toy soldier gave the tin tray a push and leapt on at the back. The tray slid down the hill.

Whoooooooosh! What a slide it was! The tray sped on over the snow like a toboggan, and carried all the toys with it. My word, what a pace it went! You should have seen it! The blue rabbit's whiskers were almost blown off.

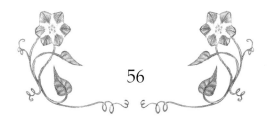

The green goblin was still staggering down the hill, deep in the snow. The tray sped after him.

"Whoooooooosh!" cried all the toys. "Look out!"

The goblin heard the noise and looked behind him. He gave a yell. The tray was almost on top of him. He tried to jump out of the way, but it wasn't any good.

Bang! The tray hit him in the back and sent him deep into the snow. He disappeared into the whiteness, and all the toys fell off the tray.

"Ooooh!" said the toy soldier.

"I've bent my whiskers," said the blue rabbit.

"Where are those bottles of sweets?" cried the bear. "Oh – here's one."

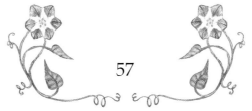

57

"And here's another!" shouted the Dutch doll, picking the second one up from the snow."

"But where's the goblin?" asked the toy soldier.

"We'd better dig him out," said the rabbit.

"Look! There are the children coming home from their walk!" cried the teddy. "We must get home quickly before they see us. Never mind the goblin!"

They all scrambled back up the hill, and in at the nursery door. They shook the snow off themselves as best they could, stood the tray in the corner, and scurried into the cupboard – only just in time!

"I can't think why our toys feel so wet," said Janet, when she opened the cupboard and took them out. "I'd very much like to know what they've been doing!"

Well, if she asked the

green goblin, she'd soon know what the toys had been up to. But, dear me, the green goblin was at the bottom of the snow! And there I'm afraid he'll have to stay till it melts. Serves him right, the naughty little thing!

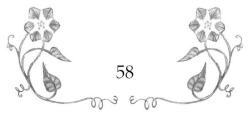

Enid Blyton

Big-Eyes the Enchanter

Big-Eyes the Enchanter had found a most marvellous spell. It was made of moonshine, starlight, the roots of mountains, the footfalls of a weasel, the breath of a fish and the smell of rain. It was stirred up with a Hoodle-Bird's tail-feather and boiled on a piece of shining ice.

It was the most powerful spell in the world. It would make Big-Eyes the Enchanter King of all the Lands on Earth. He could do what he liked. Ah, what a time he would have!

Big-Eyes was not a pleasant fellow. He didn't like flowers, he didn't like animals, he hated children. He couldn't bear fairies, he spanked every elf he met, and he hated to hear anyone laughing.

"When I use my spell and make myself King of all the Lands on Earth, I will destroy the flowers everywhere!" he cried. "I will shut all the animals up underground, and I will make all the boys and girls work hard for me from the moment they are three years old. As for the fairies and the elves, the goblins and the pixies, I'll send the whole lot to the bottom of the sea. Ho, what a time I'll have!"

He looked at the spell. It was shimmering in a great blue cauldron, stirred by his servant, a big lad with a stupid, grinning face.

Then Big-Eyes looked at his book of magic. He wanted to find out exactly when the spell would work. At last he found what he wanted to know.

"This spell when made will only act on Midsummer Day at five o'clock in the morning," he read. "Aha! Then I'll set my alarm clock for half-past four, and get the spell working at five exactly. Then thunder and lightning will come and when the spell has stopped everyone will be my slave."

The night before Midsummer Day the Enchanter set his alarm clock to go off at half-past four. Then he went to bed, full of excitement to think of all the power that would be his next day. His servant, the grinning lad, had been told to keep awake all night, and stir the spell to keep it sweet.

The Enchanter had exciting dreams. He dreamt that he was a monarch on a golden throne, set with all the rare jewels of the world. He dreamt that not a single flower blossomed on the earth. He dreamt that all the puppies and kittens, chicks and ducklings, calves and lambs were hidden away from the sunshine deep in the heart of the earth. He dreamt that all the boys and girls no longer played but worked all day long for him.

Sweet dreams for the wicked Enchanter! On he dreamt and on – and at last woke up. No alarm bell woke him – he woke up himself. He looked at

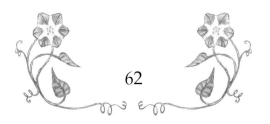

the clock. It was half past three. Not time to get up yet. He lay and waited. Then he looked at the clock again, when about half an hour had gone.

It was still half-past three. What a strange thing! The Enchanter listened for a moment – and he could hear no ticking! The clock had stopped at half-past three in the morning. He had forgotten to wind it up in his excitement the night before!

The village clock began to strike outside. One – two – three – four – five – six! Six o'clock! The right minute for the working of the spell was past! It wouldn't come again until a year was past!

In a fearful rage the Enchanter sprang out of bed. Why hadn't the servant lad warned him, when the clock had stopped? He was supposed to keep awake all night and stir the blue cauldron!

The boy was fast asleep, poor lad, his head resting on the cauldron. Big-Eyes took him by the shoulder and shook him in fury. The boy woke up in fright, and, thinking that the Enchanter was a thief come in the night, he struck out with all his might.

Biff! The Enchanter fell to the ground, and as he fell he caught at the cauldron to save himself. Sizzle-sizzle-sizzle! The shimmering spell inside upset all over him as he lay on the ground.

The servant lad watched in terror. What would his master do to him now? He would beat him, surely, or at least turn him into a frog or beetle.

The spell acted strangely. It altered the Enchanter bit by bit. He changed slowly into an old man – an old ragged man with a long ragged beard and bald head. He became a beggar-man, and slowly rose from the ground and went to stand at a corner to beg from the passers-by. And little children were sorry for him and gave him pennies.

Sometimes he remembered how he had been the great Enchanter, and then he would shake his head and mutter: "Ah! I could have ruled the world! But I forgot to wind up the clock!"

As for the servant lad, what became of him? He got such a terrible fright that he ran off to sea, and one day he told his story to me. At the end he shook his head and said: "Ah, it was a good thing my master forgot to wind up his clock that night!"

And dear me, I think it was too!

The Kickaway Shoes

Skip and Jump were very busy brownies. They had been spring-cleaning their cottage from top to bottom – and my, what a lot of rubbish they had turned out!

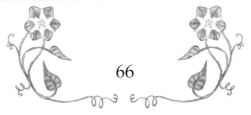

"Look at that!" said Skip, pointing to an enormous pile of old kettles, old books, and old boots and shoes he had put in their back garden. "Whatever are we going to do with all this rubbish?"

"And look at my pile of rubbish, too!" said Jump. Skip looked. It certainly was an even bigger pile than his. There was a broken-down iron bedstead, two chipped vases, an old enamel candlestick, four saucepans with holes in – oh, and heaps more things.

"What are we going to do with them?" asked Skip. "We can't burn them, they won't burn."

"And we haven't got a dustman in our village," said Jump. "So we can't ask him to collect our rubbish."

"And we are *not* going to throw these old things into the ditches, as lots of untidy people do," said Skip. "That would spoil the countryside. So what *are* we to do?"

"I say – what about borrowing those Kickaway Shoes belonging to old Grumpy Gnome!" cried Jump, all at once. "They would soon take our rubbish away!"

"Ooh, yes," said Skip. "But I'm afraid of the Grumpy Gnome. He's so bad-tempered, and I don't trust him."

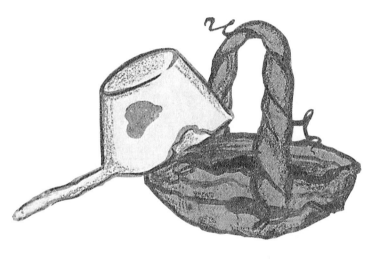

"Well, if we pay him for the loan of his magic shoes, he can't be angry with us," said Jump. "Just think, Skip! Whatever we kick with the Kickaway Shoes immediately disappears! It's wonderful! If I kicked that old saucepan there with a Kickaway Shoe, it would fly away and we'd never see it again! Ooh, it wouldn't take us long to get rid of all our rubbish then, would it?"

"And what fun it would be to do some magic kicking!" cried Skip, jumping about in excitement. "What fun! Let's go and ask Grumpy Gnome now."

"We'll take a piece of gold with us," said Jump, running to his purse, which was on the mantelpiece. "He is sure to charge us a lot. He is a greedy, selfish, horrid fellow, and nobody likes him. We won't stay long, in case he puts a nasty spell on us."

Off went the two brownies in great excitement. Jump had the piece of gold safely in his pocket. They soon came to Grumpy's cottage. It was built into the hill-side, and there was a red door with a big black knocker. Jump knocked loudly. Rat-tat-tat!

The Grumpy Gnome opened the door and glared at them. He was a nasty-looking person. He had yellow whiskers and a very long nose. His eyes were small and he wore on his head a round red cap with little silver bells all round the rim. They rang when he walked. It was a magic cap, and he never took it off, not even to brush his hair. So nobody knew whether he had any hair or not.

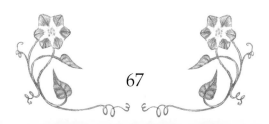

67

"What do you want?" he said, in his loud deep voice.

"Please would you lend us your Kickaway Shoes?" asked Jump politely. "We will pay you for the loan of them."

"I shall want a piece of gold," said the Grumpy Gnome, nodding his head till all the silver bells on his cap rang loudly.

"We have brought you a piece," said Jump, and he showed the gold to Grumpy. The gnome's little eyes shone at the sight of the gold, and he suddenly grabbed it and put it into his own pocket.

"Here are the shoes," he said, taking down a curious pair of shoes from a shelf behind the door. They were bright yellow, and had turned-up ends of red painted iron to kick with. The two brownies took them eagerly. They thanked the gnome and turned to go.

"Bring them back to-night without fail," commanded Grumpy. He shook his head fiercely at them. Making all the silver bells tinkle again, and then slammed the door.

"What an unpleasant creature he is, to be sure," said Skip, looking quite pale. "I was really afraid he was going to turn us into black-beetles or something! You

know, he is supposed to do that to people he doesn't like. And once he turned a cheeky pixie into a currant bun and ate him! Ooooh my, he's a horrid person!"

The brownies hurried home with the magic shoes. When they got there they each put a shoe on their right foot and danced about in glee.

"We've got the Kickaway Shoes, we've got the Kickaway Shoes!" they cried. They made such a noise that Whiskers, their big black cat, came out to see what they were doing.

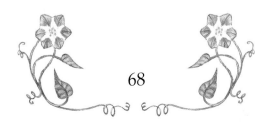

He stood behind the saucepan, lifted his right foot and gave the saucepan an enormous kick with the iron end of the Kickaway Shoe! Bang!

The saucepan shot into the air and flew away! My, how it flew! The brownies watched it going through the air until it was just a black speck. Then they couldn't see it any longer.

"I wonder where it's gone to?" said Jump.

"It's gone to the Land of Rubbish," said Skip. "Now it's your turn, Jump. Kick that vase away!"

Jump kicked with all his might. The vase broke into a hundred pieces, and each piece flew through the air at top speed.

They soon disappeared. The brownies giggled. This was great fun!

"Hello, Whiskers, darling!" cried the brownies, who were both very fond of their cat. "Look at our magic shoes."

Whiskers sniffed them and hurriedly backed away. She had smelt the magic in them and was afraid. She went off to a corner of the garden.

"Now let's start kicking away all our rubbish!" cried Skip. "Come on! Watch me kick away this old saucepan!"

"We'll both kick away this nasty old bedstead," said Skip. "It's so big it wants two people to kick it, I'm sure!"

They both kicked with all their might. At once the bedstead rose into the air, and to the great delight of the brownies, and to the enormous surprise of the pixies down in the village, the old iron bedstead flew through the air, looking smaller and

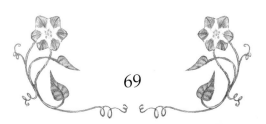

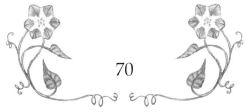

smaller the further it
flew. It was
most exciting.

The brownies laughed
till the tears came into
their eyes. They were
having a glorious time.
They kicked away the
candlesticks, the old
boots and the tin kettles.
They kicked away a pile
of books and a broken
spade. They kicked dozens of things and
shouted in glee when they saw them all
flying off in the air, never to come back.

At last there was nothing but an old
basket left. Skip gave it a hard kick, and it
rose into the air – but oh, goodness, what
a dreadful thing! Whiskers, the cat, had
curled herself up in that basket and Skip
didn't know that she was there! When the
basket rose up in the air Whiskers shot
out and she and the basket flew along
together at top speed!

Whiskers mewed loudly, but it was no
use. She had to go to the Land of
Rubbish, and soon the horrified brownies
could see nothing of her but a tiny speck
far away in the sky.

"Oh! Oh!" cried Skip, the tears running
down his cheeks in two streams. "I didn't
know Whiskers was in the basket! She'll
never come back! Oh, my dear, darling
old cat! Oh, Jump, she's gone!"

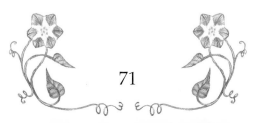

71

Jump sobbed, too. Both brownies loved their cat with all their hearts, and it was dreadful to think poor old Whiskers had been kicked off to the Land of Rubbish. How upset she would be! How lonely and frightened!

"Who will g-g-g-give her her m-m-m-m-milk?" wept Skip.

"Who will t-t-t-t-tuck her up in a warm rug at night?" sobbed Jump.

It was dreadful. The brownies couldn't think what to do! They put their arms round one another and cried so much that they made a puddle around their feet.

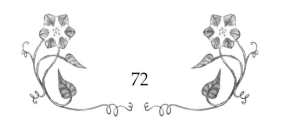

72

At last Skip had an idea.

"Let's go to Grumpy Gnome and ask him to tell us how to get Whiskers back!" he said. "There is sure to be a spell to get her back."

"Yes, yes!" cried Jump, wiping his eyes with his big yellow handkerchief. So off they set once more to Grumpy's cottage.

The gnome frowned at them when he opened the door. "I said bring back the shoes to-night, not this afternoon," he said crossly. "I was just having a nap and you've wakened me."

"Oh, please, Grumpy, we've come about something terribly important," said Skip. "We've kicked Whiskers, our lovely black cat, away by mistake, and we want you to tell us how to get her back!"

Grumpy's little eyes gleamed. "Ha!" he thought. "I can make some money out of this."

"Well," he said aloud, "that's certainly very serious. You will have to pay me a very large sum of money to get her back. It's very hard to get a black cat back from the Land of Rubbish."

"Oh dear," said Jump and Skip. "How much money do you want?"

"I want fifty pieces of gold!" said Grumpy."

"Ooooooo!" squealed Skip and Jump in horror. "We only have three pieces! Get us our cat back for three pieces, Grumpy."

"Certainly not," said the gnome, pretending that he was shutting the door. "Fifty pieces, or no cat!"

"Wait, wait!" said Jump. "We've only three pieces, I tell you. What else will you take besides our three pieces of gold?"

"Well, I'll take your grandfather clock," said Grumpy.

"Oh!" groaned the brownies sorrowfully. "We do so love our old clock. But you shall have it."

"And your rocking-chair," said Grumpy. "And the pair of lovely brass candlesticks you have on your mantlepiece."

The brownies groaned again. They were proud of their rocking-chair and candlesticks. But still, they loved Whiskers more than all these things, so they sadly promised to go back home and fetch the gold, the clock, the chair and the candlesticks at once.

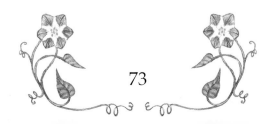

73

They ran off, crying. What a dreadful thing to have to give up all their nicest things to the horrid, greedy gnome! If he had been at all kind-hearted he would have been sorry about Whiskers, and would have got her back for nothing. But, oh, the Grumpy Gnome had a heart as hard as stone!

Skip and Jump fetched out their big clock, their old rocking-chair, and the two candlesticks. Skip had the gold in his pocket. He carried the rocking-chair, too. Jump managed to take the grandfather clock and the candlesticks. They went slowly along, panting and puffing under their heavy loads.

Just as they got near Grumpy's cottage they met Bron, the head brownie of the village. He was most astonished to see Skip and jump carrying such heavy things.

"Are you moving?" he asked.

"No," said Skip. "We are taking these things to Grumpy." Then he told Bron all that had happened, and how Grumpy had made them promise to give him their nicest things in return for getting back Whiskers from the Land of Rubbish.

"So that's why we are taking him out three gold pieces, our beautiful grand-father clock, our rocking-chair and our lovely candlesticks," said Skip sadly. "But you see, we must get Whiskers back. She'll be lonely and so frightened."

Bron frowned and looked as black as thunder when he heard about the greed and selfishness of the unkind gnome.

"Where are the Kickaway Shoes?" he asked.

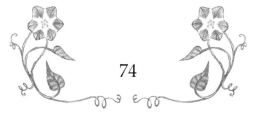

74

"I've still got one on, and so has Skip," said Jump, and he lifted up his right foot to show Bron.

"Give them to me," said Bron.

In great surprise Skip and Jump took of the Kickaway Shoes and watched Bron put them on, one on each foot.

Then they looked on in greater surprise when he marched straight up to Grumpy's front door and banged hard on the knocker.

"RAT-A-TAT-TAT!"

The door flew open and out came Grumpy, looking very angry indeed.

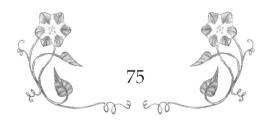

75

"How dare you knock so loudly!" he began, in a rage – then he stopped when he saw it was Bron knocking and not Skip and Jump.

"I've just come to tell you something, Grumpy Gnome," said Bron, in a very fierce voice. "I've come to tell you that you are the nastiest, greediest, unkindest gnome in the whole of the kingdom, and you don't deserve to live in this nice little village."

"Oh, don't I?" said Grumpy, his little eyes glittering wickedly. "Well, where do I deserve to live then? Tell me that!" And he turned to go indoors again.

"The best place for you is the Land of Rubbish!" shouted Bron and, before

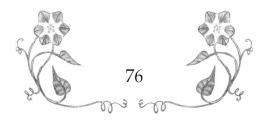

"Don't worry!" said Bron cheerfully. " A cat can always find its way home again, no matter where it's taken to. Whiskers will come back all right – and that wicked gnome knew it perfectly well. He was just robbing you of all these things for nothing. Take them back home again, put down a saucer of milk, and wait for Whiskers to come back."

"Oh, thank you, Bron," said the grateful little brownies. "But what are you going to do with the Kickaway Shoes?"

"I shall keep them in my house, and then if anyone wants to borrow them he can do so for nothing," said Bron. He put on his own shoes, and then, taking the Kickaway Shoes under his arm, he went off home, whistling loudly. He stopped every now and then to laugh when he thought of the Grumpy Gnome sailing through the air to the Land of Rubbish!

Grumpy could get inside the door, he kicked him hard with the iron points of the Kickaway Shoes – first with one shoe and then with the other.

Oh, my goodness me! Grumpy gave a loud yell and rose up into the air, and then, still yelling, he flew on and on to the Land of Rubbish. The brownies watched him – and then suddenly Skip gave a cry.

"Oh, Bron! You've kicked him away before he told us how to get back dear old Whiskers. Oh dear, oh dear!"

Skip and Jump staggered home again with all their belongings. They put them back in their places, and then they went to the larder for some milk. They poured out a saucerful,

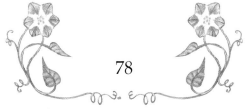

and put it down on the floor, ready for Whiskers when she came back.

Then they put the kettle on for tea, and toasted some muffins, for they really felt very hungry.

And would you believe it, just as they were sitting down to eat their tea, there came a mewing at the door! Skip leapt up and opened it – and there outside was dear old Whiskers, very tired and very hungry, for she had walked a very long way indeed.

"Darling old Whiskers!" cried the brownies in delight, hugging her and stroking her soft fur. "Oh, we are glad to see you! Here's some milk for you! And shall we open a tin of sardines for you, just for a treat?"

They were all so happy that evening. Whiskers sat on Skip's knee first, and then on Jump's, so that they might share her properly between them. She was just as glad to be back home again as they were to have her.

As for Grumpy Gnome, he's still in the Land of Rubbish. And a very good place for him, too!

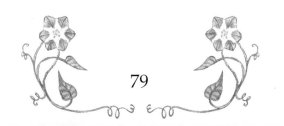

Nippy the Pixie

Nippy the pixie was a tiresome fellow. He had long strong fingers, and he loved to nip and pinch people with them. He had long toes, and he liked to kick slyly under the table. He liked to poke people too, and to tread on their toes. He was not a very pleasant fellow.

One day he was very pleased. He had an invitation to a party! It was to be a seaside party, and Nippy thought that would be most exciting. Scaly the merman had asked him to the party. Nippy felt sure he would have a fine time.

He dressed himself in his best, got on his bicycle, and rode off. It wasn't very far to the sea. He would be at the party just in time!

Scaly was there to greet him. He shook hands politely, and asked Nippy into his rock-pool, which was most beautifully decorated with seaweed and anemones.

Nippy dipped his hands into the water, rubbed them over his face, and muttered a few magic words. He could now go under the water without being wet! He could breathe there, too. It was a marvellous spell.

Nippy followed Scaly into the pool. The seaweed fluttered round. The shells made a pretty floor, laid in a neat pattern over the sand. There was a table made of rock, and on it were all sorts of exciting things to eat!

"Where are the other guests?" asked Nippy, looking round.

"They will be here in a minute," said Scaly; and, sure enough, they all swam up or crawled up as he finished speaking.

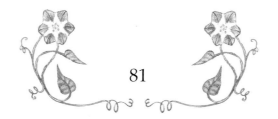

They were strange guests. There was a large yellow crab, and there were three small green crabs. There was a great lobster, a rather alarming fellow. There were six shrimps and six prawns, all neat and shining. There was a fat jellyfish with ribbons hanging down from his umbrella-like body. Nippy didn't much like the look of them.

They all knew Nippy. They shook hands with him, and nodded. "Ah, Nippy!" they said. "We have heard of you! Yes – we have heard of you!"

Nippy felt rather pleased. He hadn't known he was so famous!

"Pray, sit down!" said Scaly, the merman, beckoning his guests to the rock-table, on which there were sea-cakes, seaweed lemonade, sea-spray ice-cream with foam on the top, and rock-biscuits, hard outside and sweet inside.

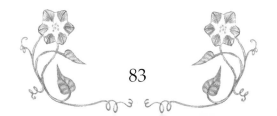

Everyone sat down. Nippy sat next to one of the little green crabs. Opposite him was the lobster. Nippy looked hungrily at the cakes. He pinched the little crab next to him in excitement. "Isn't this fun!" he said.

The crab opened a pair of his pincers and pinched Nippy back. "Ooooh!" said Nippy, startled. "Don't do that. It hurts!"

"But you did it to me," said the crab smiling, and looking at Nippy with his stalked eyes. "It's a fine game, this nipping and pinching. That's why Scaly asked you to his party – you are the only pixie he knows who can nip and pinch and poke as we can. He thought you would enjoy it very much."

"Oh," said Nippy, feeling rather alarmed.

The big lobster opposite beamed at him and put a pair of his enormous claws under the table. He felt about for Nippy's bare knee and nipped it hard.

"Ooooh!" said Nippy. "Don't!"

"You can nip me back," said the lobster. "Go on, Nippy; pinch me hard. We love it, you know."

"*We* like poking people with the sharp needles in our heads," said a large prawn suddenly to the pixie. "Like this, Nippy!"

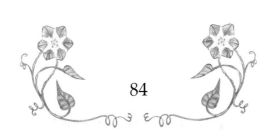

The prawn dug the surprised pixie in the chest with his sharp needle, and Nippy gave a yell and fell off his chair. Another shrimp poked him hard.

Then the big yellow crab pinched each of his toes in turn. What fun those creatures had!

"I don't like it, I don't like it!" wept Nippy. "Please stop them, Scaly."

"But this is their idea of fun," said the merman. "I thought it was yours, too, Nippy. I have often heard how you pinch, nip, kick, and poke people, so I thought you'd love my party. Please don't spoil it. Go and nip everyone else. Crabs and lobsters love that kind of game."

"But they are so hard to nip!" wept Nippy. "And they can nip me much harder than I can nip them. It isn't fair."

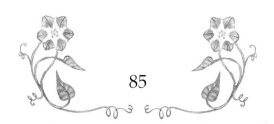

Just at that moment the jellyfish left its place and floated over to Nippy. "Play with me, pixie," it said, in a soft, shivery voice. It let down its ribbon-streamers all round the pixie, and Nippy gave a yell.

"You're stinging me, you're stinging me!" he cried. "Go away!"

"Come on, boys, let's have a fine game with this silly pixie!" cried the big lobster. And, to Nippy's horror, all the shrimps, prawns, crabs, lobster, and jellyfish surrounded him and began to have a horrid sort of game with him.

They pinched him and nipped him and pricked him and poked him and stung him till Nippy rushed out of the pool, jumped on his bicycle, and rode back home, crying bitterly.

"It was a horrid, horrid party!" he wept. "Scaly was silly to think I'd like a pinching party with all those sea-creatures!"

He sat down at home and made himself a cup of cocoa and took some biscuits from a tin, for he had had no tea at all. He thought hard as he nibbled and drank.

"I hated that pinching and poking," he thought. "How other people must have hated *my* pinching and poking too! I'll never do it again, never!"

He didn't tell anyone about Scaly's pinching party, but they all knew – because Scaly told them! How they laughed and laughed!

"Nippy won't try his old tricks again!" they said. And he didn't He keeps his fingers to himself now – and a good thing, too! If you know anyone who is a pincher or poker, just let Scaly know – he'll arrange a nice little party for them, you may be sure!

The Real Live Fairy Doll

Gwen and Peter were very much excited because they were going to have a big Christmas tree that Christmas. What fun!

"Will it have a fairy doll at the top, Mummy?" asked Gwen. "I do hope it will."

"You shall have a fairy doll at the very top!" said Mummy, "and lots of toys and candles all over the tree."

That night Daddy and Mummy went out to buy the tree and all the things to hang on it. They bought the prettiest fairy doll you ever saw, with wings of silver, and a dress that shone and glittered. She was to go at the top of the tree.

All the toys were hung on the tree, and the candles were slipped into their stands and clipped to the branches. The doll was fastened to the very tip, and how grand she looked, shining there. Mummy and Daddy were very pleased.

The toys in the nursery sat and looked at the tree in delight, when Mummy and Daddy had gone downstairs. They thought they had never in all their life seen such a pretty thing. As for the fairy doll, they thought she was the loveliest toy in the world.

Then a most dreadful thing happened. What do you think? The poor fairy doll was not fastened tightly enough to the tree, and suddenly she felt herself falling!

"Help! Help!" she squealed.

But nobody could help her. She fell – she slid between the branches of the Christmas tree and landed with a bump on the floor.

All the toys rushed to pick her up.

But oh, dear me, she had broken both her nice little legs! What a dreadful thing!

"Whatever shall we do?" said the teddy bear. "Is there time for her to be mended before the children have the tree tomorrow night?"

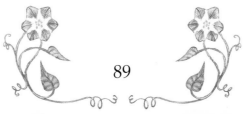

"Let's go and ask the elf who lives under the nursery window," said the toy soldier. "She knows a lot. Perhaps she could mend the fairy doll."

So they called her in. She came dancing into the nursery and looked at the poor broken doll crying on the floor.

"I will take her to the Mend-Up Gnome," she said. "He will soon mend her nicely. She will be quite all right in twenty-four hours' time."

"Twenty-four hours!" cried the toys. "Goodness, won't the children be disappointed. They *did* so want a fairy doll to stand at the top of their Christmas tree tomorrow night!"

Everyone stood looking very gloomy – and then the toy soldier spoke up. He turned to the elf and said: "I say! Would *you* take the fairy doll's place do you think? You have silvery wings like hers and your dress is all shiny and glittering too. You would have a fine time at the top of the tree and you would see everything that was going on."

"Well," said the elf, thoughtfully, "well – let me see. Yes – I think I could do that for you. I love boys and girls and it would be fun to see them all dancing round the tree and having their presents. I'll just take this doll to old Mend-Up, and then I'll come back and fly up to the top of the tree!"

You should have seen how lovely she looked up there! The toys looked and looked at her – and when the party began the next day, how all the children stared to see such a beautiful fairy doll at the top of the tree!

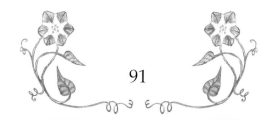

"It's a real, live fairy; that's what it is," said another little girl. "It's not a doll at all!"

She had a lovely time. She watched the children dancing – and do you know what she did when the grown-ups had gone out of the room to have some supper, and had left the children by themselves? She flew down from the tree, took hands with them and danced all round the tree, singing a little magic song in a high, silvery voice.

The children were surprised and pleased.

"I say! That's a wonderful fairy doll of yours!" said one little girl to Gwen. "My doll talks and walks, but I've never seen one that could dance and sing!"

Just then the elf heard the grown-ups coming and she flew straight back to the top of the tree.

"Mummy!" cried Gwen. "Do you know, the fairy doll flew down from the tree and danced and sang with us!"

"Nonsense!" said Mummy, and nobody would believe that what the children said was true.

"Well," said Gwen to Peter, "when Mummy takes the fairy doll down from the tree to-morrow, she will find it is a real live fairy – and won't she be surprised?"

But the little fairy doll came back from Mend-Up the Gnome's that night, both her legs beautifully mended, and the toys helped her to climb to the top of the tree. The elf flew down and said good-bye to the toys.

"I *have* enjoyed myself!" she said. "And wasn't it fun when I flew down and danced with the children? I nearly laughed out loud to see their surprised faces!"

The next day the children begged their mother to take down the fairy doll from the tree. They felt quite sure it was a *real* fairy, and not a doll. But when they saw her, what a disappointment!

"It's a doll after all!" said Gwen. "I wonder how it was she turned into a live fairy last night."

"Don't be silly," said Mummy, laughing. "I don't know why you keep telling that foolish story, Gwen. No fairy doll could come down from the tree and dance and sing."

"Well, it *must* have been a fairy then," said Peter. "So that settles it!"

He was quite right, wasn't he?

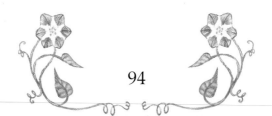

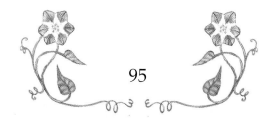